THE SONG
SENTIMENTAL BLOKE

By C·J·DENNIS

With Illustrations by Hal Gye

ETT Imprint

Exile Bay

This Imprint Classics edition published by ETT Imprint, 2024
First electronic edition ETT Imprint 2017

ETT IMPRINT
PO Box R1906
Royal Exchange NSW 1225
Australia

Illustrated edition copyright © ETT Imprint Pty Ltd, 1995, 2017
Hal Gye images copyright © ETT Imprint 1995, 2017
Introduction copyright © John Derum 2022

First published by Angus & Robertson 1915
Facsimile reprint 1957, 1958, 1960, 1962 (twice), 1963, 1964, 1965, 1967, 1969, 1980,1986, 1990
Imprint paperback edition 1993, 1995, 2021
Imprint Classics edition 2024

ISBN 978-1-923024-82-3 (pbk)
ISBN 978-1-922698-12-4 (ebk)

Cover: Hal Gye

Designed by Tom Thompson

To
Mr and Mrs J.G. Roberts

To
Mr and Mrs J.G. Roberts

INTRODUCTION

How terrific that this collection of poems is being printed again more than a hundred years after its first publication.

Bill, the Sentimental Bloke, first appeared in the weekly magazine *The Bulletin* in 1909.

The first use of the term "The Sentimental Bloke" comes as the title for a group of four of the poems published in Dennis's collection *Backblock Ballads and Other Verses* in 1913. Then in 1915 *The Songs Of A Sentimental Bloke* was published containing all the previously published poems and some new.

When Dennis asked Henry Lawson to write an introduction to the original publication of *The Songs of A Sentimental Bloke* he described his endeavour:

"I have tried to tell a common but very beautiful story in coarse language, to prove amongst other things that life and love can be just as real and splendid to the "common" bloke as to the "cultured". I have tried to deal with primitive passions and phases that occur in every man's life. And I have tried to show the poor blind snobs that beautiful thoughts are quite possible amongst the vulgar whom they affect to despise and pity."

Lawson's introduction is included here and yet correspondence in the papers of the publisher George Robertson reveals that Lawson wanted to include the above passage but Dennis preferred his "author's voice " was not present in the introduction, only in the verses.

Although from a very different time, Bill is a familiar character and his thoughts and reflections are recognisable. When they first met the Bloke, Australians were involved in one the numerous international wars and conflicts of the twentieth century and had not yet experienced the influenza epidemic that started in 1918 and the massive social and economic changes that followed through the twentieth century. In 1915 Australia had very few telephones, indeed very little electricity, and certainly none of the electric and electronic forms of communication that emerged in the twentieth and twenty-first centuries. Radio and television were dreams for the future.

And yet the thoughts, aspirations and melancholy of this sentimental bloke will be as recognisable to any computer programmer, flight controller, or radiographer as they were to every market gardener, factory worker and shearer.

The Bloke is not the earliest larrikin character in our literature, but for more than a hundred years he has been the most identifiable and with the other major characters in his life — his mate, Ginger Mick and the love of his life, Doreen — they have become part of our language.

And although far from the first use of idiom and slang in poetry, it was the slang, the poor spelling and grammar that upset a few conservative folk. The book was barred from their households by some including, I was told, my own grandfather.

Nevertheless, it appealed to the rebellious in young people whose children, later in the twentieth century, would become known as "teenagers".

Some of the slang words and phrases were not actually in common use but had been gathered by Dennis in his travels. It was part of the enjoyment, as with any slang or secret language, to know the lingo. With the inclusion of Dennis's witty glossary in subsequent editions (the glossary was not included in the first edition) many of those words and phrases have come into common usage and are part of our language.

I understand from people who remembered the time, that the poems were often read or recited in living rooms, pubs and around campfires. And I still think they are best enjoyed aloud — even if read aloud to one's self!

Would the Bloke be different if he was to be written about in this century?

Perhaps he would have emerged in popular song rather than verse. Again, facilitated by the development of the relevant technology. The social challenges of this century are more sophisticated and complex perhaps, but the personal issues are very much the same.

I like to think that Dennis would have expanded on the compassion he showed for Aboriginal Australians and migrants in his later poems such as "Black Peter Myloh", "The Melting Pot" and "The Spoilers". The original Australians are rarely present in the works of 19th and early 20th century Australian writing, and even more rarely in a positive light. Certainly, we can see here Dennis's understanding of our natural environment and its care — an issue that became a major concern for him in later years.

I have always loved Dennis's choice of "Songs" rather than a less lyrical description of his poems.

Bill, of course, never refers to himself as "sentimental". The word doesn't actually appear in any of the poems. A twenty-first century counsellor or therapist might readily be able to identify any number of conditions and syndromes to explain Bill's thoughts and moods but Dennis allows Bill to puzzle over the highs and lows, the joys and regrets of being alive and takes us on what we might now call his journey or the arc of his growth.

JOHN DERUM
Sydney 2022

FOREWORD

MY young friend Dennis has honoured me with a request to write a preface to his book. I think a man can best write a preface to his own book, provided he knows it is good. Also if he knows it is bad.

The Sentimental Bloke, while running through the *Bulletin*, brightened up many dark days for me. He is more perfect than any alleged "larrikin" or Bottle-O character I have ever attempted to sketch, not even excepting my own beloved Benno. Take the first poem for instance, where the Sentimental Bloke gets the hump. How many men, in how many different parts of the world — and of how many different languages — have had the same feeling — the longing for something better — to be something better?

The exquisite humour of *The Sentimental Bloke* speaks for itself; but there's a danger that its brilliance may obscure the rest, especially for minds, of all stations, that, apart from sport and racing, are totally devoted to boiling

"The cabbitch storks or somethink"
in this social "pickle found-ery" of ours.

Doreen stands for all good women, whether down in the smothering alleys or up in the frozen heights.

And so, having introduced the little woman (they all seem "little" women), I "dips me lid" — and stand aside.

HENRY LAWSON

SYDNEY, 1st September, 1915.

CONTENTS

A vie est vaine:
Un peu d'amour,
Un peu de haine . . .
Et puis-bonjour!

La vie est breve:
Un peu d'espoir,
Un peu de reve . . .
Et puis-bonsoir!

LEON MONTENAEKEN

I.   A SPRING SONG

A Spring Song

HE world 'as got me snouted jist a treat;
  Crool Forchin's dirty left 'as smote me soul;
An' all them joys o' life I 'eld so sweet
  Is up the pole.
Fer, as the poit sez, me 'eart 'as got
  The pip wiv yearnin' fer — I dunno wot.

I'm crook; me name is Mud; I've done me dash;
  Me flamin' spirit's got the flamin' 'ump!
I'm longin' to let loose on somethin' rash....
  Aw, I'm a chump!
I know it; but this blimed ole Springtime craze

  Fair outs me, on these dilly, silly days.

The young green leaves is shootin' on the trees,
  The air is like a long, cool swig o' beer,
The bonzer smell o' flow'rs is on the breeze,
  An' 'ere's me, 'ere,
Jist moochin' round like some pore, barmy coot,
Of 'ope, an' joy, an' forchin destichoot.

I've lorst me former joy in gettin' shick,
  Or 'eadin' browns; I 'aven't got the 'eart
To word a tom; an', square an' all, I'm sick
  Of that cheap tart
'Oo chucks 'er carkis at a feller's 'ead
An' mauls 'im ...Ar! I wish't that I wus dead! ...

Ther's little breezes stirrin' in the leaves,
  An' sparrers chirpin' 'igh the 'ole day long;
An' on the air a sad, sweet music breaves
  A bonzer song —
A mournful sorter choon thet gits a bloke
Fair in the brisket 'ere, an' makes 'im choke ...

What is the matter wiv me? ...   I dunno.
  I got a sorter yearnin' 'ere   inside,
A dead-crook sorter thing that won't let go
  Or be denied —
A feelin' like I want to do a break,
An' stoush creation for some woman's sake.

The little birds is chirpin' in the nest,
  The parks an' gardings is a bosker sight,
Where smilin' tarts walks up an' down, all dressed
  In clobber white.
An', as their snowy forms goes steppin' by,
It seems I'm seekin' somethin' on the sly.

Somethin' or someone — I don't rightly know;
  But, seems to me, I'm kind er lookin' for
A tart I knoo a 'undred years ago,
  Or, maybe, more.
Wot's this I've 'eard them call that thing? ...Geewhizz!
Me ideel bit o' skirt! That's wot it is!

Me ideel tart! ... An', bli'me, look at me!
  Jist take a squiz at this, an' tell me can
Some square an' honist tom take this to be
  'Er own true man?
Aw, Gawd! I'd be as true to 'er, I would —
As straight an' stiddy as ...   Ar, wot's the good?

Me, that 'as done me stretch fer stoushin' Johns,
  An' spen's me leisure gittin' on the shick,
An' 'arf me nights down there, in Little Lon.,
  Wiv Ginger Mick,
Jist 'eadin' 'em, an' doing in me gilt.
Tough luck! I s'pose it's 'ow a man is   built.

It's 'ow Gawd builds a bloke; but don't it 'urt
  When 'e gits yearnin's fer this 'igher life,
On these Spring mornin's, watchin' some sweet skirt —
  Some fucher wife —
Go sailin' by, an' turnin' on his phiz
The glarssy eye — fer bein' wot 'e is.

I've watched 'em walkin' in the gardings 'ere —
  Cliners from orfices an' shops an' such;
The sorter skirts I dursn't come too near,
  Or dare to touch.
An, when I see the kind er looks they carst ...
Gorstrooth! Wot is the use o' me, I arst?

Wot wus I slung 'ere for? An' wot's the good
  Of yearnin' after any ideel tart?
Ar, if a bloke wus only understood!
  'E's got a 'eart:
'E's got a soul inside 'im, poor or rich.
But wot's the use, when 'Eaven's crool'd 'is pitch?

I tells meself some day I'll take a pull
  An' look eround fer some good, stiddy job,
An' cut the push fer good an' all; I'm full
  Of that crook mob!
An', in some Spring the fucher 'olds in store,
I'll cop me prize an' long in vain no more.

The little winds is stirrin' in the trees,
  Where little birds is chantin' lovers' lays;
The music of the sorft an' barmy breeze....
  Aw, spare me days!
If this 'ere dilly feelin' doesn't stop
I'll lose me block an' stoush some flamin' cop!

II. THE INTRO

The Intro

'R name's Doreen... Well, spare me bloomin'
    days!
You could er knocked me down wiv 'arf a
    brick!
Yes, me, that kids meself I know their
    ways,
An' 'as a name for smoogin' in our click!

I just lines up an' tips the saucy wink.
But strike! The way she piled on dawg! Yer'd think
  A bloke was givin' back-chat to the Queen....
    'Er name's Doreen.

I seen 'er in the markit first uv all,
Inspectin' brums at Steeny Isaacs' stall.
  I backs me barrer in — the same ole way —
  An' sez, "Wot O! It's been a bonzer day.
'Ow is it fer a walk?" ... Oh, 'oly wars!
The sorter look she gimme! Jest becors
  I tried to chat 'er, like you'd make a start
    Wiv any tart.

An' I kin take me oaf I wus perlite,
An' never said no word that wasn't right,
  An' never tried to maul 'er, or to do
  A thing yeh might call crook. Ter tell yeh true,
I didn't seem to 'ave the nerve — wiv 'er.
I felt as if I couldn't go that fur,
  An' start to sling off chiack like I used ...
    Not intrajuiced!

Nex' time I sighted 'er in Little Bourke,
Where she was in a job. I found 'er lurk
  Wus pastin' labels in a pickle joint,
    A game that — any'ow, that ain't the point.
Once more I tried ter chat 'er in the street,
But, bli'me! Did she turn me down a treat!
  The way she tossed 'er 'ead an' swished 'er skirt!
        Oh, it wus dirt!

A squarer tom, I swear, I never seen,
In all me natchril, than this 'ere Doreen.
  It wer'n't no guyver neither; fer I knoo
  That any other bloke 'ad Buckley's 'oo
Tried fer to pick 'er up. Yes, she was square.
She jist sailed by an' lef' me standin' there
  Like any mug. Thinks I, "I'm out er luck,"
        An' done a duck.

Well, I dunno. It's that way wiv a bloke.
If she'd ha' breasted up ter me an' spoke,
  I'd thort 'er jist a commin bit er fluff,
  An' then fergot about 'er, like enough.
It's jest like this. The tarts that's 'ard ter get
Makes you all 'ot to chase 'em, an' to let
  The cove called Cupid get an 'ammer-lock;
        An' lose yer block.

I know a bloke 'oo knows a bloke 'oo toils
In that same pickle found-ery. ('E boils
  The cabbitch storks or somethink.) Anyway,
  I gives me pal the orfis fer to say
'E 'as a sister in the trade 'oo's been
Out uv a jorb, an' wants ter meet Doreen;
  Then we kin get an intro, if we've luck.
        'E sez, "Ribuck."

O' course we worked the oricle; you bet!
But, 'struth, I ain't recovered frum it yet!
  'Twas on a Saturdee, in Colluns Street,
  An' — quite by accident, o' course — we meet.
Me pal 'e trots 'er up an' does the toff- '
Eallus wus a bloke fer showin' off.
    "This 'ere's Doreen," 'e sez. "This 'ere's the Kid."
        I dips me lid.

"This 'ere's Doreen," 'e sez. I sez "Good day."
An', bli'me, I 'ad nothin' more ter say!
  I couldn't speak a word, or meet 'er eye.
  Clean done me block! I never been so shy,
Not since I was a tiny little cub,
An' run the rabbit to the corner pub —
  Wot time the Summer days wus dry an' 'ot —
        Fer me ole pot.

Me! that 'as barracked tarts, an' torked an' larft,
An' chucked orf at 'em like a phonergraft!
  Gorstrooth! I seemed to lose me Pow'r o' speech.
  But, 'er! Oh, strike me pink! She is a peach!
The sweetest in the barrer! Spare me days,
I carn't describe that diner's winnin' ways.
  The way she torks! 'Er lips! 'Er eyes! 'Er hair! ...
        Oh, gimme air!

I dunno 'ow I done it in the end.
I reckerlect I arst ter be 'er   friend;
  An' tried ter play at 'andies in the   park,
  A thing she wouldn't sight. Aw, it's a nark!
I gotter swear when I think wot a mug
I must 'a' seemed to 'er. But still I 'ug
  That promise that she give me fer the beach.
        The bonzer peach!

Now, as the poit sez, the days drag by
On ledding feet. I wish't they'd do a guy.
  I dunno 'ow I 'ad the nerve ter speak,
  An' make that meet wiv 'er fer Sundee week!
But strike! It's funny wot a bloke'll do
When 'e's all out. ...   She's gorn, when I come-to.
  I'm yappin' to me cobber uv me mash....
        I've done me dash!

'Er name's Doreen.... An' me — that thort I knoo
The ways uv tarts, an' all that smoogin' game!
  An' so I ort; fer ain't I known a few?
  Yet some'ow ...I dunno. It ain't the same.
I carn't tell wot it is; but, all I know,
I've dropped me bundle-an' I'm glad it's so.
  Fer when I come ter think uv wot I been....
        'Er name's Doreen.

III.   THE STOUSH O' DAY

The Stoush o' Day

R, these is 'appy days! An' 'ow they've flown —
   Flown like the smoke of some inchanted fag;
   Since dear Doreen, the sweetest tart I've known,
Passed me the jolt that made me sky the rag.

An' ev'ry golding day Roats o'er a chap
Like a glad dream of some celeschil scrap.

Refreshed wiv sleep Day to the momin' mill
  Comes jauntily to out the nigger, Night.
Trained to the minute, confident in skill,
  'E swaggers in the East, chock-full o' skite;
Then spars a bit, an' plugs Night on the point.
Out go the stars; an' Day 'as jumped the joint.

The sun looks up, an' wiv a cautious stare,
  Like some crook keekin' o'er a winder sill
To make dead cert'in everythink is square,
  'E shoves 'is boko o'er an Eastern 'ill,
Then rises, wiv 'is dial all a-grin,
An' sez, " 'Ooray! I knoo that we could win!"

Sure of 'is title then, the champeen Day
  Begins to put on dawg among 'is push,
An', as he mooches on 'is gaudy way,
  Drors tribute from each tree an' flow'r an' bush.
An', w'ile 'e swigs the dew in sylvan bars,
The sun shouts insults at the sneakin' stars.

Then, lo! the push o' Day rise to applaud;
  An' all 'is creatures clamour at 'is feet
Until 'e thinks 'imself a little gawd,
  An' swaggers on an' kids 'imself a treat.
The w'ile the lurkin' barrackers o' Night
Sneak in retreat an' plan another fight.

On thro' the hours, triumphant, proud an' fit,
  The champeen marches on 'is up'ard way,
Till, at the zenith, bli'me! 'E-is-IT!
  And all the world bows to the Boshter Day.
The jealous Night speeds ethergrams thro' space
'Otly demandin' terms, an' time, an' place.

A w'ile the champeen scorns to make reply;
  'E's taken tickets on 'is own 'igh worth;
Puffed up wiv pride, an' livin' mighty 'igh,
  'E don't admit that Night is on the earth.
But as the hours creep on 'e deigns to state
'E'll fight for all the earth an' 'arf the gate.

Late afternoon ... Day feels 'is Habby arms,
  An' tells 'imself 'e don't seem quite the thing.
The 'omin' birds shriek clamorous alarms;
  An' Night creeps stealthily to gain the ring.
But see! The champeen backs an' fills, becos
'E doesn't feel the Boshter Bloke 'e was.

Time does a bunk as us-u-al, nor stays
  A single instant, e'en at Day's be'est.
Alas, the 'eavy-weight's 'igh-livin' ways
  'As made 'im soft, an' large around the vest.
'E sez 'e's fat inside; 'e starts to whine;
'E sez 'e wants to dror the colour line.

Relentless nigger Night crawls thro' the ropes,
    Advancin' grimly on the quakin' Day,
Whose noisy push, shorn of their 'igh-noon 'opes,
    Wait, 'ushed an' anxious, fer the comin' fray.
And many lusty barrackers of noon
Desert 'im one by one — traitors so soon!

'E's out er form! 'E 'asn't trained enough!
    They mark their sickly champeen on the stage,
An' narked, the sun, 'is backer, in a huff,
    Sneaks outer sight, red in the face wiv rage.
W'ile gloomy roosters, they 'oo made the morn
Ring wiv 'is praises, creep to bed forlorn.

All faint an' groggy grows the beaten Day;
    'E staggers drunkenly about the ring;
An owl 'oats jeerin'ly across the way,
    An' bats come out to mock the fallin' King.
Now, wiv a jolt, Night spreads 'im on the Boor,
An' all the west grows ruddy wiv 'is gore.

A single, vulgar star leers from the sky
    An' in derision, rudely mutters, "Yah!"
The moon, Night's conkerbine, comes glidin' by
    An' laughs a 'eartless, silvery "Ha-ha!"
Scorned, beaten, Day gives up the 'opeless fight,
An' drops 'is bundle in the lap o' Night.

So goes each day, like some celeschil mill,
    E'er since I met that shyin' little peach.
'Er bonzer voice! I 'ear its music still,
    As when she guv that promise fer the beach.
An', square an' all, no matter 'ow yeh start,
The commin end of most of us is — Tart.

IV.   DOREEN

Doreen

WISH'T yeh meant it, Bill." Oh, 'ow me 'eart
   Went out to 'er that ev'nin' on the beach.
I knoo she weren't no ordinary tart,
   My little peach!
I tell yeh, square an' all, me 'eart stood still
To 'ear 'er say, "I wish't yeh meant it, Bill."

To 'ear 'er voice! Its gentle sorter tone,
   Like soft dream-music of some Dago band.
An' me all out; an' 'oldin' in me own
     'Er little 'and.
An' 'ow she blushed!
O, strikef it was divine
The way she raised 'er shinin' eyes to mine.

'Er eyes! Soft in the moon; such boshter eyes!
   An' when they sight a bloke ... O, spare me days!
'E goes all loose inside; such glamour lies
     In 'er sweet gaze.
It makes 'im all ashamed uv wot 'e's been
To look inter the eyes of my Doreen.

The wet sands glistened, an' the gleamin' moon
   Shone yeller on the sea, all streakin' down.
A band was playin' some soft, dreamy choon;
     An' up the town
We 'eard the distant tram-cars whir an' clash.
An' there I told 'er 'ow I'd done me dash.

"I wisq't yeh meant it." 'Struth! And did I, fair?
  A bloke 'ud be a dawg to kid a skirt
Like 'er. An' me well knowin' she was square.
      It 'ud be dirt!
'E'd be no man to point wiv 'er, an' kid.
I meant it honest; an' she knoo I did.

She knoo. I've done me block in on 'er, straight.
  A cove 'as got to think some time in life
An' get some decent tart, ere it's too late,
      To be 'is wife.
But, Gawd! 'Oo would 'a' thort it could 'a' been
My luck to strike the likes of 'er? ... Doreen!

Aw, I can stand their chuckin' off, I can.
  It's 'ard; an' I'd delight to take 'em on.
The dawgs! But it gets that way wiv a man
      When 'e's fair gone.
She'll sight no stoush; an' so I 'ave to take
Their mag, an' do a duck fer 'er sweet sake.

Fer 'er sweet sake I've gone and chucked it clean:
  The pubs an' schools an' all that leery game.
Fer when a bloke 'as come to know Doreen,
      It ain't the same.
There's 'igher things, she sez, for blokes to do.
An' I am 'arf believin' that it's true.

Yes, 'igher things — that wus the way she spoke;
  An' when she looked at me I sorter felt
That bosker feelin' that comes o'er a bloke,
      An' makes 'im melt;
Makes 'im all 'ot to maul 'er, an' to shove
'Is arms about 'er ... Bli'me? but it's love!

That's wot it is. An' when a man 'as grown
  Like that 'e gets a sorter yearn inside
To be a little 'ero on 'is own;
          An' see the pride
Glow in the eyes of 'er 'e calls 'is queen;
An' 'ear 'er say 'e is a shine champeen.

"I wish't yeh meant it," I can 'ear 'er yet,
   My bit o' Huff! The moon was shinin' bright,
Tumin' the waves all yeller where it set-
          A bonzer night!
The sparklin' sea all sorter gold an' green;
An' on the pier the band — O, 'Ell! ...   Doreen!

V. THE PLAY

The Play

OT'S in a name?" she sez . . . An' then she sighs,
  An' clasps 'er little 'ands, an' rolls 'er eyes.
  "A rose," she sez, "be any other name
  Would smell the same.
Oh, w'erefore art you Romeo, young sir?
Chuck yer ole pot, an' change yer moniker!"

Doreen an' me, we bin to see a show —
Theswell two-dollar touch. Bong tong, yeh know.
A chair apiece wiv velvit on the seat;
A slap-up treat.
The drarmer's writ be Shakespeare, years ago,
About a barmy goat called Romeo.

"Lady, be yonder moon I swear!" sez 'e.
An' then 'e climbs up on the balkiney;
An' there they smooge a treat, wiv pretty words
Like two love-birds.
I nudge Doreen. She whispers, "Ain't it grand!"
'Er eyes is shinin'; an' I squeeze 'er 'and.

"Wot's in a name?" she sez. 'Struth, I dunno.
Billo is just as good as Romeo.
She may be Juli-er or Juli-et —
'E loves 'er yet.
If she's the tart 'e wants, then she's 'is queen,
Names never count ...   But ar, I like "Doreen!"

36

A sweeter, dearer sound I never 'eard;
Ther's music 'angs around that little word,
Doreen! ... But wot was this I starts to say
About the play?
I'm off me beat. But when a bloke's in love
'Is thorts turns 'er way, like a 'omin' dove.

This Romeo 'e's lurkin' wiv a crew —
A dead tough crowd o' crooks — called Montague.
 'Is diner's push-wot's nicknamed Capulet —
They 'as 'em set.
Fair narks they are, jist like them back-street clicks,
Ixcep' they fights wiv skewers 'stid o' bricks.

Wot's in a name? Wot's in a string o' words?
They scraps in ole Verona wiv the'r swords,
An' never give a bloke a stray dog's chance,
An' that's Romance.
But when they deals it out wiv bricks an' boots
In Little Lon., they're low, degraded broots.

Wot's jist plain stoush wiv us, right 'ere to-day,
Is "valler" if yer fur enough away.
Some time, some writer bloke will do the trick
Wiv Ginger Mick,
Of Spadger's Lane. '*E'll* be a Romeo,
When 'e's bin dead five 'undred years or so.

Fair Juli-et, she gives 'er boy the tip.
Sez she: "Don't sling that crowd o' mine no lip;
An' if you run agin a Capulet,
Jist do a get."
'E swears 'e's done wiv lash; 'e'll chuck it clean.
(Same as I done when I first met Doreen.)

They smooge some more at that. Ar, strike me blue!
It gimme Joes to sit an' watch them two!
'E'd break away an' start to say good-bye,
An' then she'd sigh
"Ow, Ro-me-o!" an' git a strangle-holt,
An' 'ang around 'im like she feared 'e'd bolt.

Nex' day 'e words a gorspil cove about
A secret weddin'; an' they plan it out.
'E spouts a piece about 'ow 'e's bewitched:
Then they git 'itched ...
Now, 'ere's the place where I fair git the pip!
She's 'is for keeps, an' yet 'e lets 'er slip!

Ar! but 'e makes me sick! A fair gazob!
'E's jist the glarsey on the soulful sob,
'E'll sigh and spruik, an' 'owl a love-sick vow —
(The silly cow!)
But when 'e's got 'er, spliced an' on the straight
'E crools the pitch, an' tries to kid it's Fate.

Aw! Fate me foot! Instid of slopin' soon
As 'e was wed, off on 'is 'oneymoon,
'Im an' 'is cobber, called Mick Curio,
They 'ave to go
An' mix it wiv that push o' Capulets.
They look fer trouble; an' it's wot they gets.

A tug named Tyball (cousin to the skirt)
Sprags 'em an' makes a start to sling off dirt.
Nex' minnit there's a reel ole ding-dong go —
'Arf round or so.
Mick Curio, 'e gets it in the neck,
"Ar rats!" 'e sez, an' passes in 'is check.

Quite natchril, Romeo gits wet as 'ell
"It's me or you!" 'e 'owls, an' wiv a yell,
Plunks Tyball through the gizzard wiv 'is sword,
'Ow I ongcored!
"Put in the boot!" I sez. "Put in the boot!"
"'Ush!" sez Doreen ... "Shame!" sez some silly coot.

Then Romeo, 'e dunno wot to do.
The cops gits busy, like they allwiz do,
An' nose around until 'e gits blue funk
An' does a bunk.
They wants 'is tart to wed some other guy.
"Ah, strike!" she sez. "I wish that I could die!"

Now, this 'ere gorspil bloke's a fair shrewd 'ead.
Sez 'e "I'll dope yeh, so they'll think yer dead."
(I tips 'e was a cunnin' sort, wot knoo
A thing or two.)
She takes 'is knock-out drops, up in 'er room:
They think she's snuffed, an' plant 'er in 'er tomb.

Then things gits mixed a treat an' starts to whirl.
'Ere's Romeo comes back an' finds 'is girl
Tucked in 'er little coffing, cold an' stiff,
An' in a jiff,
'E swallows lysol, throws a fancy fit,
'Ead over turkey, an' 'is soul 'as flit

Then Juli-et wakes up an' sees 'im there,
Tums on the water-works an' tears 'er 'air,
"Dear love," she sez, "I cannot live alone!"
An' wiv a moan,
She grabs 'is pockit knife, an' ends 'er cares ...
"Peanuts or lollies!" sez a boy upstairs.

VI.   THE STROR 'AT COOT

· HAL· GYE ·

The Stor 'at Coot

 R wimmin! Wot a blinded fool I've been!
I arsts meself, wot else could I ixpeck?
I done me block complete on this Doreen,
    An' now me 'eart is broke, me life's a
        wreck!
The dreams I dreamed, the dilly thorts I thunk
Is up the pole, an' joy 'as done a bunk.

Wimmin! O strike! I orter known the game!
    Their tricks is crook, their arts is all dead snide.
The 'ole world over tarts is all the same;
    All soft an' smilin' wiv no 'eart inside.
But she fair doped me wiv 'er winnin' ways,
Then crooled me pitch fer all me mortal days.

They're all the same! A man 'as got to be
    Stric' master if 'e wants to snare 'em sure.
'E 'as to take a stand an' let 'em see
    That triffin' is a thing 'e won't indure.
'E wants to show 'em that 'e 'olds command,
So they will smooge an' feed out of 'is 'and.

'E needs to make 'em feel 'e is the boss,
    An' kid 'e's careless uv the joys they give.
'E 'as to make 'em think 'e'll feel no loss
    To part wiv any tart 'e's trackin' wiv.
That all their pretty ways is crook pretence
Is plain to any bloke wiv common-sense.

But when the birds is nestin' in the spring,
    An' when the soft green leaves is in the bud,
'E drops 'is bundle to some Huffy thing.
    'E pays 'er 'omage — an' 'is name is Mud.
She plays wiv 'im an' kids 'im on a treat,
Until she 'as 'im crawlin' at 'er feet.

An' then, when 'e's fair orf 'is top wiv love,
    When she 'as got 'im good an' 'ad 'er fun,
She slings 'im over like a carst-orf glove,
    To let the other tarts see wot she's done.
All vanity, deceit an' 'eartless kid!
I orter known; an', spare me days, I did!

I knoo. But when I looked into 'er eyes —
    Them shinin' eyes o' blue all soft wiv love —
Wiv *mimic* love — they seemed to 'ipnertize.
    I wus content to place 'er 'igh above.
I wus content to make of 'er a queen;
An' so she seemed them days ... O, 'struth!... Doreen!

I knoo. But when I stroked 'er glossy 'air
    Wiv rev'rint 'ands, 'er cheek pressed close to mine,
Me lonely life seemed robbed of all its care;
    I dreams me dreams, an' 'ope begun to shine.
An' when she 'eld 'er lips fer me to kiss ...
Ar, wot's the use? I'm done wiv all o' this!

Wimmin! ... Oh, I ain't jealous! Spare me days!
  Me? Jealous uv a knock-kneed coot like that!
'Im! Wiv 'is cute stror 'at an' pretty ways!
  I'd be a mug to squeal or whip the cat.
I'm glad, I am — glad 'cos I know I'm free!
There ain't no call to tork o' jealousy.

I tells meself I'm well out o' the game;
  Fer look, I mighter married 'er — an' then....
Ar strike! 'Er voice wus music when my name
  Wus on 'er lips on them glad ev'nin's when
We useter meet. An' then to think she'd go ...
No, I ain't jealous — but — Ar, I dunno!

I took a derry on this stror 'at coot
  First time I seen 'im dodgin' round Doreen.
'Im, wiv 'is giddy tie an' Yankee soot,
  Ferever yappin' like a tork-machine
About "The Hoffis" where 'e 'ad a grip...
They 'e smiled at 'er give me the pip!

She sez I stoushed 'im, when I promised fair
  To chuck it, even to a friendly spar.
Stoushed 'im! I never roughed 'is pretty 'air!
  I only spanked 'im gentle, fer 'is mar.
If I'd 'a' jabbed 'im once, there would 'a' been
An inquest; an' I sez so to Doreen.

I mighter took an' cracked 'im in the street,
  When she was wiv 'im there lars' Fridee night.
But don't I keep me temper when we met?
  An' don't I raise me lid an' act perlite?
I only jerks me elbow in 'is ribs,
To give the gentle office to 'is nibs.

Stoushed 'im! I owns I met 'im on the quiet,
    An' worded 'im about a small   affair;
An' when 'e won't put up 'is 'ands to fight —
    ('E sez, "Fer public brawls 'e didn't care") —
I lays 'im 'cross me knee, the mother's joy,
An' smacks 'im 'earty, like a naughty boy.

An' now Doreen she sez I've broke me vow,
    An' mags about this coot's pore, "wounded pride."
An' then, o' course, we 'as a ding-dong row,
    Wiv 'ot an' stormy words on either side.
She sez I done it outer jealousy,
An' so, we parts fer ever — 'er an' me.

Me jealous? Jealous of that cross-eyed cow
    I set 'im 'cos I couldn't sight 'is face.
'Is yappin' fair got on me nerves, some'ow.
    I couldn't stand 'im 'angin' round 'er place.
A coot like that! ... But it don't matter much,
She's welkim to 'im if she fancies such.

I swear I'll never track wiv 'er no more;
    I'll never look on 'er side o' the street —
Unless she comes an' begs me pardin for
    Them things she said to me' in angry 'eat.
She can't ixpeck fer me to smooge an' crawl.
I ain't at any woman's beck an' call.

Wimmin! I've took a tumble to their game.
    I've got the 'ole bang tribe o' diners set!
The 'ole world over they are all the same:
    Crook to the core the bunch of 'em — an' yet
We could 'a' been that 'appy, 'er an' me ...
But, wot's it matter? Ain't I glad I'm free?

A bloke wiv commin-sense 'as got to own
    There's little 'appiness in married life.
The smoogin' game is better left alone,
    Fer tarts is few that makes the ideel wife.
An' them's the sort that loves wivout disguise,
An' thinks the sun shines in their 'usban's' eyes.

But when the birds is matin' in the spring,
    An' when the tender leaves begin to bud,
A feelin' comes — a dilly sorter thing —
    That seems to sorter swamp 'im like a flood.
An' when the fever 'ere inside 'im burns,
Then freedom ain't the thing fer wot 'e yearns.

But I 'ave chucked it all. An' yet — I own
    I dreams me dreams when soft Spring breezes stirs;
An' often, when I'm moonin' 'ere alone,
    A lispin' maid, wiv 'air an' eyes like 'ers,
'Oo calls me "dad," she climbs upon me knee,
An' yaps 'er pretty baby tork to me.

I sorter see a little 'ouse, it seems,
    Wiv someone waitin' for me at the gate ...
Ar, where's the sense in dreamin' barmy dreams,
    I've dreamed before, and nearly woke too late.
Sich 'appiness could never last fer long,
We're strangers — 'less she owns that she was wrong.

To call 'er back I'll never lift a 'and;
    She'll never 'ear £rum me by word or sign.
Per'aps, some day, she'll come to understand
    The mess she's made o' this 'ere life o' mine.
Oh, I ain't much to look at, I admit.
But 'im! The knock-kneed, swivel-eyed misfit? ...

VII.   THE SIREN

The Siren

 HE sung a song; an' I sat silent there,
　　Wiv bofe 'ands grippin' 'ard on to me chair;
　　　Me 'eart, that yesterdee I thort wus broke
　　Wiv 'umpin' sich a 'eavy load o' care,
　　　Come swellin' in me throat like I would
　　　　　choke.
I felt 'ot blushes climbin' to me 'air.

'Twas like that feelin' when the Spring wind breaves
Sad music in the sof'ly rustlin' leaves.
　　An' when a bloke sits down an' starts to chew
Crook thorts, wivout quite knowin' why 'e grieves
　　Fer things 'e's done 'e didn't ort to do —
Fair winded wiv the 'eavy sighs 'e 'eaves.

She sung a song; an' orl at once I seen
The kind o' crool an' 'eartless broot I been.
　　In ev'ry word I read it like a book —
The slanter game I'd played wiv my Doreen —
　　I 'eard it in 'er song; an' in 'er look
I seen wot made me feel fair rotten mean.

Poor, 'urt Doreen! My tender bit o' fluff!
Ar, men don't understand; they're fur too rough;
　　Their ways is fur too coarse wiv lovin' tarts;
They never gives 'em symperthy enough.
　　They treats 'em 'arsh; they tramples on their 'earts,
Becos their own crool 'earts is leather-tough.

She sung a song; an' orl them bitter things
That chewin' over lovers' quarrils brings
   Guv place to thorts of sorrer an' remorse.
Like when some dilly punter goes an' slings
   'Is larst, lone deener on some stiffened 'orse,
An' learns them vain regrets wot 'urts an' stings.

'Twas at a beano where I lobs along
To drown them memories o' fancied wrong.
   I swears I never knoo that she'd be there.
But when I met 'er eye — O, 'struth, 'twas strong!
   Twas bitter strong, that jolt o' dull despair!
'Er look o' scorn! ... An' then, she sung a song.

The choon was one o' them sad, mournful things
That ketch yeh in the bellers 'ere, and brings
   Tears to yer eyes. The words was uv a tart
'Oo's trackin' wiv a silly coot 'oo slings
   'Er love aside, an' breaks 'er tender 'eart ...
But 'twasn't that; it was the way she sings.

To 'ear 'er voice! ... A bloke 'ud be a log
'Oo kep' 'is block. Me mind wus in a fog
   Of sorrer for to think 'ow I wus wrong;
Ar, I 'ave been a fair ungrateful 'og!
   The feelin' that she put into that song
'Ud melt the 'eart-strings of a chiner dog.

I listens wiv me 'eart up in me throat;
I drunk in ev'ry word an' ev'ry note.
   Tears trembles in 'er voice when she tells 'ow
That tart snuffed out becos 'e never wrote.
   An' then I seen 'ow I wus like that cow.
Wiv suddin shame me guilty soul wus smote.

Doreen she never looked my way; but stood
'Arf turned away, an' beefed it out reel good,
    Until she sang that bit about the grave;
"Too late 'e learned 'e 'ad misunderstood!"
    An' then — Gorstrooth! The pleadin' look she gave
Fair in me face 'ud melt a 'eart o' wood.

I dunno 'ow I seen that evenin' thro'.
They muster thort I was 'arf shick, I knoo.
    But I 'ad 'urt Doreen wivout no call;
I seen me dooty, wot I 'ad to do.
    O, strike! I could 'a' blubbed before 'em all!
But I sat tight, an' never cracked a boo.

An' when at larst the tarts they makes a rise,
A lop-eared coot wiv 'air down to 'is eyes
    'E 'oaks on to Doreen, an' starts to roam
Fer 'ome an' muvver. I lines up an' cries,
    "'An's orf! I'm seein' this 'ere diner 'ome!"
An' there we left 'im, gapin' wiv surprise.

She never spoke; she never said no word;
But walked beside me like she never 'eard.
    I swallers 'ard, an' starts to coax an' plead,
I sez I'm dead ashamed o' wot's occurred.
    She don't reply; she never takes no 'eed;
Jist stares before 'er like a startled bird.

I tells 'er, never can no uvver tart
Be 'arf wot she is, if we 'ave to part.
    I tells 'er that me life will be a wreck. It ain't no go.
But when I makes a start
    To walk away, 'er arms is roun' me   neck.
"Ah, Kid!" she sobs. "Yeh nearly broke me 'eart!"

I dunno wot I done or wot I   said.
But 'struth! I'll not forgit it till I'm dead —
   That night when 'ape back in me brisket lobs:
'Ow my Doreen she lays 'er little   'ead
   Down on me shoulder 'ere, an' sobs an' sobs;
An' orl the lights goes sorter blurred an' red.

Say, square an' all — It don't seem right, some'ow,
To say such things; but wot I'm feelin' now
   'As come at times, I s'pose, to uvver men —
When you 'ave 'ad a reel ole ding-dong row,
   Say, ain't it boozer makin' up agen?
Straight wire, it's almost worth ... Ar, I'm a cow!

To think I'd ever seek to 'arm a 'air
Of 'er dear 'ead agen! My oath, I swear
   No more I'll roust on 'er in angry 'eat!
But still, she never seemed to me so fair;
   She never wus so tender or so sweet
As when she smooged beneath the lamplight there.

She's never been so lovin' wiv 'er gaze;
So gentle wiv 'er pretty wimmin's ways.
   I tells 'er she's me queen, me angel, too.
"Ah, no, I ain't no angel, Kid," she   says.
   "I'm jist a woman, an' I loves yeh true!
An' so I'll love yeh all me mortal days!"

She sung a song ... 'Ere, in me barmy style,
I sets orl tarts; for in me hour o' trile
   Me soul was withered be a woman's frown,
An' broodin' care come roostin' on me dile.
   She sung a song ... Me 'eart, wiv woe carst down,
Wus raised to 'Eaven be a woman's smile

VIII.   MAR

Mar

"R pore dear Par," she sez, "'e kept a store";
　　An' then she weeps an' stares 'ard at the floor.
　　　"'T was thro' 'is death," she sez, "we wus
　　　　rejuiced
　　To this," she sez , . . An' then she weeps
　　　some more.

"'Er Par," she sez, "me poor late 'usband, kept
An 'ay an' corn store. 'E'd no faults ixcept
　　'Im fallin' 'eavy orf a load o' char
W'ich — killed 'im — on the — " 'Struth! But 'ow she wept.

She blows 'er nose an' sniffs." 'E would 'a' made"
She sez "a lot of money in the trade.
　　But, 'im took orf so sudden-like, we found
'E 'adn't kept 'is life insurince paid.

'To think," she sez, "a child o' mine should be
Rejuiced to workin' in a factory!
　　If 'er pore Par 'e 'adn't died," she sobs ...
I sez, "It wus a bit o' luck for me."

Then I gits red as 'ell, "That is — I mean,"
I sez, "I mighter never met Doreen
　　If 'e 'ad not" — an' 'ere I lose me block —
"I 'ope," I sez, "'e snuffed it quick and clean."

An' that wus 'ow I made me first deboo.
I'd dodged it cunnin' fer a month or two.
　　Doreen she sez, "You'll 'ave to meet my Mar,
Some day," she sez. An' so I seen it thro'.

I'd pictered some stem female in a cap
Wot puts the fear o' Gawd into a chap.
    An' 'ere she wus, aweepin' in 'er tea
An' drippin' moistcher like a leaky tap.

Two dilly sorter dawgs made outer delf
Stares 'ard at me frum orf the mantelshelf.
    I seemed to symperthise wiv them there pups;
I felt so stiff an' brittle-like meself.

Clobber? Me trosso, 'ead to foot, wus noo —
Got up regardless, fer this interview.
    Stiff shirt, a Yankee soot split up the back,
A tie wiv yeller spots an' stripes o' blue.

Me cuffs kep' playin' wiv me nervis fears
Me patent leathers nearly brought the tears
    An' there I sits wiv, "Yes, mum. Thanks. Indeed?"
Me stand-up collar sorin' orf me ears.

"Life's 'ard," she sez, an' then she brightens up.
"Still, we 'ave alwus 'ad our bite and sup.
    Doreen's been *sich* a help; she 'as indeed.
Some more tea, Willy? 'Ave another cup."

Willy! O 'ell! 'Ere wus a flamin' pill!
A moniker that alwus makes me ill.
    "If it's the same to you, mum," I replies
"I answer quicker to the name of Bill."

Up goes 'er 'ands an' eyes, "That vulgar name!"
No, Willy, but it isn't all the same,
My fucher son must be respectable."
"Orright," I sez, "I s'pose it's in the game."

"Me fucher son," she sez, "right on frum this
Must not take anythink I say amiss.
   I know me jooty be me son-in-lor;
So, Willy, come an' give yer Mar a kiss."

I done it. Tho' I dunno 'ow I did.
"Dear boy," she sez, "to do as you are bid.
   Be kind to 'er," she sobs, "my little girl!"
An' then I kiss Doreen. Sez she "Ah Kid!"

Doreen! Ar 'ow 'er pretty eyes did shine.
No sight on earth or 'Eaving's 'arf so fine,
   An' as they looked at me she seemed to say
"I'm proud of 'im, I am, an' 'e is mine."

There wus a sorter glimmer in 'er eye,
An 'appy, nervis look, 'arf proud, 'arf shy;
   I seen 'er in me mind be'ind the cups
In our own little kipsie, bye an' bye.

An' then when Mar-in-lor an' me began
To tork of 'ouse'old things an' scheme an' plan,
   A sudden thort fair jolts me where I live:
"These is my wimmin folk! An' I'm a man!"

It's wot they calls responsibility.
All of a 'eap that feelin' come to me;
   An' somew'ere in me 'ead I seemed to feel
A sneakin' sort o' wish that I was free.

'Ere's me 'oo never took no 'eed o' life,
Investin' in a mar-in-lor an' wife:
   Someone to battle fer besides meself,
Somethink to love an' shield frum care and strife.

It makes yeh solim when yeh come to think
Wot love and marridge means. Ar, strike me pink!
    It ain't all sighs and kisses. It's yer life.
An' 'ere's me tremblin' on the bloomin' brink.

"'Er pore dead Par," she sez, an' gulps a sob.
An' then I tells 'er 'ow I got a job,
    As storeman down at Jones' printin' joint,
A decent sorter cop at fifty bob.

Then things get 'ome-like; an' we torks till late,
An' tries to tease Doreen to fix the date,
    An' she gits suddin soft and tender-like,
An' cries a bit, when we parts at the gate.

An' as I'm moochin' 'omeward frum the car
A suddin notion stops me wiv a jar —
    Wot if Doreen, I thinks, should grow to be,
A fat ole weepin' willer like 'er Mar!

O, 'struth! It won't bear thinkin' of! It's crook!
An' I'm a mean, unfeelin' dawg to look
    At things like that. Doreen's Doreen to me,
The sweetest peach on w'ich a man wus shook.

'Er "pore dear Par" ... I s'pose 'e 'ad 'is day,
An' kissed an' smooged an' loved 'er in 'is way.
    An' wed an' took 'is chances like a man —
But, Gawd, this splicin' racket ain't all   play.

Love is a gamble, an' there ain't no certs.
Some day, I s'pose, I'll git wise to the skirts,
    An' learn to take the bitter wiv the sweet ...
But, strike me purple! "Willy!" That's wot 'urts.

IX. PILOT COVE

Pilot Cove

"OUNG friend," 'e sez ...Young friend!
     Well, spare me days!
   Yeh'd think I wus 'is own white-'eaded boy —
The queer ale finger, wiv 'is gentle ways.
"Young friend," 'e sez, "I wish't yeh bofe great joy."
The langwidge that them parson blokes imploy
Fair tickles me. The way 'e bleats an' brays!
     "Young friend," 'e sez.

"Young friend," 'e sez ...   Yes, my Doreen an' me
  We're gettin' hitched, all straight an' on the square.
Fer when I torks about the registry —
  O 'oly wars! yeh should 'a' seen 'er stare;
  "The registry?" she sez, "I wouldn't dare!
I know a clergyman we'll go an' see" ...
    "Young friend," 'e sez.

"Young friend," 'e sez. An' then 'e chats me straight;
  An' spouts of death, an' 'ell, an' mortal sins.
"You reckernize this step you contemplate
  Is grave?" 'e sez. An' I jist stan's an' grins;
  Fer when I chips, Doreen she kicks me shins.
"Yes, very 'oly is the married state,
    Young friend," 'e sez.

"Young friend," 'e sez. An' then 'e mags a lot
  Of jooty an' the spiritchuil life,
To which I didn't tumble worth a jot.
  "I'm sure," 'e sez, "as you will 'ave a wife
  'Oo'll 'ave a noble inB'ince on yer life.
'Oo is 'er gardjin?" I sez, "'Er ole pot" —
    "Young friend!" 'e sez.

"Young friend," 'e sez. "Oh fix yer thorts on 'igh!
　Orl marridges is registered up　there!
An'　you must cleave unto 'er till　yeh die,
　An' cherish 'er wiv love an' tender care.
　E'n　in　the days when　she's no longer fair
She's still yer wife," 'e sez. "Ribuck," sez I.
　　　　"Young friend!" 'e sez.

"Young friend," 'e sez — I sez, "Now, listen 'ere:
　This isn't one o' them impetchus leaps.
There ain't no tart a 'undreth　part so　dear
　As 'er. She 'as me 'eart an' soul fer keeps!"
　An'　then Doreen, she turns away an'　weeps;
But 'e jist smiles. "Yer deep in love, 'tis clear,
　　　　Young friend," 'e sez.

"Young friend," 'e sez — an' tears wus in 'is eyes —
　"Strive 'ard. Fer many, many years I've lived.
An' I kin but recall wiv tears an'　sighs
　The　lives of　some I've seen　in　marridge gived."
　"My Gawd!" I sez. "I'll strive as no bloke strivved!
Fer don't I know I've copped a bonzer prize?"
　　　　"Young friend," 'e　sez.

"Young friend," 'e sez. An' in 'is gentle way,
　'E pats the shoulder of my dear　Doreen.
"I've solem'ized grand weddin's in me day,
　But 'ere's the sweetest little maid I've seen.
　She's fit fer any man, to be 'is queen;
An' you're more forchinit than you kin say,
　　　　Young friend," 'e sez.

"Young friend," 'e sez ... A queer ole pilot bloke,
   Wiv silver 'air. The gentle way 'e dealt
Wiv 'er, the soft an' kindly way 'e spoke
   To my Doreen, 'ud make a statcher melt.
   I tell yer, square an' all, I sorter felt
A kiddish kind o' feelin' like I'd choke ...
       "Young friend," 'e sez.

"Young friend," 'e sez, "you two on Choosday week,
   Is to be joined in very 'oly bonds.
To break them vows I 'opes yeh'll never seek;
   Fer I could curse them 'usbands 'oo absconds!"
   "I'll love 'er till I snuff it," I responds.
"Ah, that's the way I likes to 'ear yeh speak,
       Young friend," 'e sez.

"Young friend," 'e sez — an' then me 'and 'e grips —
   "I wish't yeh luck, you an' yer lady fair.
Sweet maid." An' sof'ly wiv 'is finger-tips,
   'E takes an' strokes me cliner's shinin' 'air.
   An' when I seen 'er standin' blushin' there,
I turns an' kisses 'er, fair on the lips.
       "Young friend!" 'e sez.

X.   HITCHED

Hitched

"N'—wilt—yeh—take—this—woman—fer—to—
be—
    Yer—weddid—wife?" . . . O, strike me!
        Will I wot?
Take 'er? Doreen? 'E stan's there *arstin'* me!
As if 'e thort per'aps I'd rather not!
Take 'er? 'E seemed to think 'er kind was got
Like cigarette-cards, fer the arstin'. Still,
  I does me stunt in this 'ere hitchin' rot,
An' speaks me piece: "Righto!" I sez, "I will."

"I will," I sez. An' tho' a joyful shout
  Come from me bustin' 'eart — I know it did —
Me voice got sorter mangled comin' out,
  An' makes me whisper like a frightened kid.
  "I will," I squeaks. An' I'd 'a' give a quid
To 'ad it on the quite, wivout this fuss,
  An' orl the starin' crowd that Mar 'ad bid
To see this solim hitchin' up of us.

"Fer—rich—er—er—fer—por—er." So 'e bleats.
  "In—sick—ness—an'—in—'ealth," ... An' there I stands,
An' dunno 'arf the chatter I repeats,
  Nor wot the 'ell to do wiv my two 'ands.
  But 'e don't 'urry puttin' on our brands —
This white-'aired pilot-bloke-but gives it lip,
  Dressed in 'is little shirt, wiv frills an' bands.
"In sick-ness—an'—in—" Ar! I got the pip!

An' once I missed me turn; an' Ginger Mick,
  'Oo's my best-man, 'e ups an' beefs it out.
"I will!" 'e 'owls; an' fetches me a kick.
  "Your turn to chin!" 'e tips wiv a shout.
  An' there I'm standin' like a gawky lout.
(Aw, spare me! But I seemed to be *all* 'ands!)
  An' wonders wot 'e's goin' crook about,
Wiv 'arf a mind to crack 'im where 'e stands.

O, lumme! But ole Ginger was a trick!
  Got up regardless fer the solim rite.
('E 'awks the bunnies when 'e toils, does Mick)
  An' twice I saw 'im feelin' fer a light
  To start a fag; an' trembles lest 'e might,
Thro' force o' habit like. 'E's nervis too;
  That's plain, fer or! 'is air o' bluff an' skite;
An' jist as keen as me to see it thro'.

But," 'struth, the wimmin! 'Ow they love this frill!
  Fer Auntie Liz, an' Mar, o' course, wus there;
An' Mar's two uncles' wives, an' Cousin Lil,
  An' 'arf a dozen more to grin and stare.
  I couldn't make me 'ands fit anywhere!
I felt like I wus up afore the Beak!
  But my Doreen she never turns a 'air,
Nor misses once when it's 'er turn to speak.

Ar, strike! No more swell marridges fer me!
　　It seems a blinded year afore 'e's done.
We could 'a' fixed it in the   registree
　　Twice over 'fore this cove 'ad 'arf begun.
　　I s'pose the wimmin git some sorter fun
Wiv all this guyver, an' 'is nibs's shirt.
　　But, seems to me, it takes the bloomin' bun,
This stylish splicin' uv a bloke an' skirt.

"To—be—yer—weddid—wife—" Aw, take a pull!
　　Wot in the 'ell's 'e think I come there for?
An' so 'e drawls an' drones until I'm full,
　　An' wants to do a duck clean out the door.
　　An' yet, fer orl 'is 'igh-falutin' jor,
Ole Snowy wus a reel good-meanin' bloke.
　　If 'twasn't fer the 'oly look 'e wore
Yeh'd think 'e piled it on jist fer a joke.

An', when at last 'e shuts 'is little book,
　　I 'eaves a sigh that nearly bust me vest.
But 'Eavens! Now 'ere's muvver goin' crook!
　　An' sobbin' awful on me manly chest!
　　(I wish she'd give them water-works a rest.)
"My little girl!" she 'owls. "O, treat 'er well!
　　She's young-too young to leave 'er muvver's nest!"
"Orright, ole chook," I nearly sez. Oh, 'ell!

An' then we 'as a beano up at Mar's —
    A slap-up feed, wiv wine an' two big geese.
Doreen sits next ter me, 'er eyes like stars.
        O, 'ow I wished their blessed yap would cease!
    The Parson-bloke 'e speaks a little piece,
That makes me blush an' 'ang me silly 'ead.
    'E sez 'e 'opes our lovin' will increase —
I *likes* that pilot fer the things 'e said.

'E sez Doreen an' me is in a boat,
    An' sailin' on the matrimonial sea.
'E sez as 'ow 'e 'opes we'll allus float
    In peace an' joy, from storm an' danger free.
    Then muvver gits to weepin' in 'er tea;
An' Auntie Liz sobs like a winded colt;
    An' Cousin Li! comes 'round an' kisses me;
Until I feel I'll *'ave* to do a bolt.

Then Ginger gits end-up an' makes a speech —
    ('E'd 'ad a couple, but 'e wasn't shick.)
"My cobber 'ere," 'e sez, "'as copped a peach!
    Of orl the barrer-load she is the pick!
    I 'opes 'e won't fergit 'is pals too quick
As wus 'is frien's in olden days, becors,
    I'm trustin', later on," sez Ginger Mick,
"To celebrate the chris'nin'." ... 'Oly wars!

At last Doreen an' me we gits away,
    An' leaves 'em doin' nothin' to the scran.
(We're honey-moonin' down beside the Bay.)
    I gives a 'arf a dollar to the   man
    Wot drives the cab; an' like two kids we ran
To ketch the train — Ah, strike! I could 'a' flown!
    We gets the carridge right agen the van.
She whistles, jolts, an' starts ... An' we're alone!

Doreen an' me! My precious bit o' fluff!
    Me own true weddid wife! ... An' we're alone!
She seems so frail, an' me so big an' rough —
    I dunno wot this feelin' is that's grown
    Inside me 'ere that makes me feel I own
A thing so tender like I fear to squeeze
    Too 'ard fer fear she'll break ... Then, wiv a groan
I starts to 'ear a coot call, "Tickets, please!"

You could 'a' outed me right on the spot!
    I wus so rattled when that porter spoke.
Fer, 'struth! them tickets I 'ad fair forgot!
    But 'e jist laughs, an' takes it fer a joke.
    'We must ixcuse," 'e sez, "new-married folk."
An' I pays up, an' grins, an' blushes red....
    It shows 'ow married life improves a bloke:
If I'd bin single I'd 'a' punched 'is head!

XI.   BEEF TEA

Beef Tea

HE never magged; she never said no word;
  But sat an' looked at me an' never stirred.
    I could 'a' bluffed it out if she 'ad been
Fair narked, an' let me 'ave it wiv 'er tongue;
But silence told me 'ow 'er 'eart wus wrung.
        Poor 'urt Doreen!

Gorstruth! I'd sooner fight wiv fifty men
Than git one look like that frum 'er agen!

She never moved; she never spoke no word;
That 'urt look in 'er eyes, like some scared bird:
    "'Ere is the man I loved," it seemed to say.
"'E's mine, this crawlin' thing, an' I'm 'is wife;
Tied up fer good; an' or! me joy in life
        Is chucked away!"
If she 'ad bashed me I'd 'a felt no 'urt!
But 'ere she treats me like — like I wus dirt.

'Ow is a man to guard agen that look?
Fer other wimmin, when the'r blokes go crook,
    An' lobs 'ome wiv the wages uv a jag,
They smashes things an' carries on a treat
An' 'owls an' scolds an' wakes the bloomin' street
        Wiv noisy mag.
But 'er — she never speaks; she never stirs ...
I drops me bundle ... An' the game is 'ers.

Jist two months wed! Eight weeks uv married bliss
Wiv my Doreen, an' now it's come to this!
   Wot wus I thinkin' uv? Gawd! I ain't fit
To kiss the place 'er little feet 'as been!
'Er that I called me wife, me own Doreen!
      Fond dreams 'as flit;
Love's done a bunk, an' joy is up the pole;
An' shame an' sorrer's roostin' in me soul.

'Twus orl becors uv Ginger Mick — the cow!
(I wish't I 'ad 'im 'ere to deal wiv now!
   I'd pass 'im one, I would! 'E ain't no man!)
I meets 'im Choosdee ev'nin' up the town.
"Wot O," 'e chips me. "Kin yeh keep one down?"
     I sez I can.
We 'as a couple; then meets three er four
Flash coves I useter know, an' 'as some more.

"'Ow are yeh on a little gamble, Kid?"
Sez Ginger Mick. "Lars' night I'm on four quid.
   Come 'round an' try yer luck at Steeny's school."
"No," sez me conscience. Then I thinks, 'Why not?
An' buy 'er presents if I wins a pot?
     A blazin' fool
I wus. Fer 'arf a mo' I 'as a fight;
Then conscience skies the wipe ... Sez I "Orright."

Ten minutes later I was back once more,
Kip in me 'and, on Steeny Isaac's floor,
   Me luck was in an' I wus 'eadin' good.
Yes, back agen amongst the same old crew!
An' orl the time down in me 'eart I knew
      I never should ...
Nex' thing I knows it's after two o'clock —
Two in the mornin'! An' I've done me block!

"Wot odds?" I thinks. 'Tm in fer it orright."
An' so I stops ari' gambles orl the night;
   An' bribes me conscience wiv the gilt I wins.
But when I comes out in the cold, 'ard dawn
I know I've crooled me pitch; me soul's in pawn.
     My flamin' sins
They 'its me in a 'eap right where I live;
Fer I 'ave broke the solim vow I give.

She never magged; she never said no word.
An' when I speaks, it seems she never 'eard.
   I could 'a' sung a nim, I feels so gay!
If she 'ad only roused I might 'a' smiled.
She jist seems 'urt an' crushed; not even riled.
    I turns away,
An' yanks me carkis out into the yard,
Like some whipped pup; an' kicks meself reel 'ard.

An' then, I sneaks to bed, an' feels dead crook.
Fer golden quids I couldn't face that look —
 That trouble in the eyes uv my Doreen.
Aw, strike! Wot made me go an' do this things?
I feel jist like a chewed up bit of string,
  An' rotten mean!
Fer 'arf an hour I lies there feelin' cheap;
An' then I s'pose, I muster fell asleep....

"'Ere, Kid, drink this" ... I wakes, an' lifts me 'ead,
An' sees 'er standin' there beside the bed;
 A basin in 'er 'ands; an' in 'er eyes —
(Eyes that wiv unshed tears is shinin' wet) —
The sorter look I never shall ferget,
  Until I dies.
"'Ere, Kid, drink this," she sez, an' smiles at me.
I looks — an' spare me days! It was beef tea!

Beef tea! She treats me like a hinvaleed!
Me! that 'as caused 'er lovin' 'eart to bleed.
 It 'urts me worse than maggin' fer a week!
'Er! 'oo 'ad right to turn dead sour on me,
Fergives like that, an' feeds me wiv beef tea ...
  I tries to speak;
An' then — I ain't ashamed o' wot I did —
I 'ides me face ... an' blubbers like a kid.

XII.   UNCLE JIM

Uncle Jim

GOT no time fer wasters, lad," sez 'e,
    "Give me a man wiv grit," sez Uncle Jim.
'E bores 'is cute ole eyes right into me,
    While I stares 'ard an' gives it back to 'im.
Then orl at once 'e grips me 'and in 'is:
"Some'ow," 'e sez, "I likes yer ugly phiz."

"You got a look," 'e sez, "like you could stay;
    Altho' yeh mauls King's English when yeh yaps,
An' 'angs flash frills on ev'rythink yeh say.
    I ain't no grammarist meself, per'aps,
But langwidge is a 'elp, I owns," sez Unk,
"When things is goin' crook." An' 'ere 'e wunk.

"Yeh'll find it tough," 'e sez, "to knuckle down.
    Good farmin' is a gift — like spoutin' slang.
Yeh'll 'ave to cut the luxuries o' town,
    An' chuck the manners of this back-street gang;
Fer country life ain't cigarettes and beer."
'Tm game," I sez. Sez Uncle, "Put it 'ere!"

Like that I took the plunge, an' slung the game.
    I've parted wiv them joys I 'eld most dear;
I've sent the leery bloke that bore me name
    Clean to the pack wivout one pearly tear;
An' frum the ashes of a ne'er-do-well
A bloomin' farmer's blossomin' like 'ell.

Farmer! That's me! Wiv this 'ere strong right 'and
   I've gripped the plough; and blistered jist a treat.
Doreen an' me 'as gone upon the land.
   Yours truly fer the burden an' the 'eat!
Yours truly fer upendin' chunks o' soil!
The 'ealthy, 'ardy, 'appy son o' toil!

I owns I've 'ankered fer me former joys;
   I've 'ad me hours o' broodin' on me woes;
I've missed the comp'ny, an' I've missed the noise,
   The football matches an' the picter shows.
I've missed — but, say, it makes me feel fair mean
To whip the cat; an' then see my Doreen.

To see the colour comin' in 'er cheeks,
   To see 'er eyes grow brighter day be day,
The new, glad way she looks an' laughs an' speaks
   Is worf ten times the things I've chucked away.
An' there's a secret, whispered in the dark, '
As made me 'eart sing like a flamin' lark.

Jist let me tell yeh 'ow it come about.
   The things that I've been thro' 'ud fill a book.
Right frum me birf Fate played to knock me out;
   The 'and that I 'ad dealt to me was crook!
Then comes Doreen, an' patches up me parst;
Now Forchin's come to bunk wiv me at larst.

First orf, one night poor Mar gits suddin fits,
    An' floats wivout the time to wave "good-byes."
Doreen is orl broke up the day she flits;
    It tears me 'eart in two the way she cries.
To see 'er grief, it almost made me glad
I never knowed the mar I must 'ave 'ad.

We done poor Muvver proud when she went out —
    A slap-up send-orf, trimmed wiv tears an' crape.
An' then fer weeks Doreen she mopes about,
    An' life takes on a gloomy sorter shape.
I watch 'er face git pale, 'er eyes grow dim;
Till — like some 'airy angel — comes ole Jim.

A cherub togged in sunburn an' a beard
    An' duds that shouted "'Ayseed!" fer a mile:
Care took the count the minute 'e appeared,
    An' sorrer shrivelled up before 'is smile,
'E got the 'ammer-lock on my good-will
The minute that 'e sez, "So, this is Bill."

It's got me beat. Doreen's late Par, some way,
    Was second cousin to 'is bruvver's wife.
Somethin' like that. In less than 'arf a day
    It seemed 'e'd been my uncle orl me life.
'E takes me 'and: "I dunno 'ow it   is,"
'E sez, "but, lad, I likes that ugly phiz."

An' when 'e'd stayed wiv us a little while
  The 'ouse begun to look like 'ome once more.
Doreen she brightens up beneath 'is smile,
  An' 'ugs 'im till I kids I'm gettin' sore.
Then, late one night, 'e opens up 'is scheme,
An' passes me wot looks like some fond dream.

'E 'as a little fruit-farm, doin' well;
  'E saved a tidy bit to see 'im thro';
'E's gittin' old fer toil, an' wants a spell;
  An' 'ere's a 'ome jist waitin' fer us two.
"It's 'ers an' yours fer keeps when I am gone,"
Sez Uncle Jim. "Lad, will yeh take it on?"

So that's the strength of it. An' 'ere's me now
  A flamin' berry farmer, full o' toil;
Playin' joo-jitsoo wiv an' 'orse an' plough,
  An' coaxin' fancy tucker frum the soil,
An' lor.gin', while I wrestles with the rake,
Fer days when me poor back fergits to ache.

Me days an' nights is full of schemes an' plans
  To figger profits an' cut out the loss;
An' when the pickin's on, I 'ave me 'an's
  To take me orders while I act the boss;
It's sorter sweet to 'ave the right to rouse ...
An' my Doreen's the lady of the 'ouse.

84

To see 'er bustlin' 'round about the place,
    Full of the simple joy o' doin' things,
That thoughtful, 'appy look upon 'er face,
    That 'ope an' peace an' pride o' labour brings,
Is worth the crowd of joys I knoo one time,
An' makes regrettin' 'em seem like a crime.

An' ev'ry little while ole Uncle Jim
    Comes up to stay a bit an' pass a tip.
It gives us 'eart jist fer to look at 'im,
    An' feel the friendship in 'is warm 'and-grip.
'Im, wiv the sunburn on 'is kind ole dile;
'Im, wiv the sunbeams in 'is sweet ole smile.

"I got no time fer wasters, lad," sez 'e,
    "But that there ugly mug o' yourn I trust."
An' so I reckon that it's up to me
    To make a bloomin' do of it or bust.
I got to take the back-ache wiv the rest,
An' plug along, an' do me little best.

Luck ain't no steady visitor, I know;
    But now an' then it calls — fer look at me!
You wouldn't take me, 'bout a year ago,
    Free gratis wiv a shillin' pound o' tea;
Then, in a blessed 'eap, ole Forchin lands
A missus an' a farm fair in me 'ands.

XIII.   THE KID

The Kid

M Y son! ... Them words, jist like a blessed
      song,
Is singin' in me 'eart the 'ole day long;
    Over an' over; while I'm scared I'll wake
    Out of a dream, to find it all a fake.

My son! Two little words, that, yesterdee,
Wus jist two simple, senseless words to me;
    An' now — no man, not since the world begun,
    Made any better pray'r than that.... My son!

My son an' bloomin' 'eir ... Ours! ... 'Ers an' mine!
The finest kid in — Aw, the sun don't shine —
    Ther' ain't no joy fer me beneath the blue
    Unless I'm gazin' lovin' at them two.

A little while ago it was jist "me" —
A lonely, longin' streak o' misery.
    An' then 'twas "'er an' me" — Doreen, my wife!
    An' now it's" 'im an' us" an' — sich is life.

But 'struth! 'E is king-pin! The 'ead serang!
I mustn't tramp about, or talk no slang;
    I mustn't pinch 'is nose, or make a face,
    I mustn't — Strike! 'E seems to own the place!

Cunnin'? Yeh'd think, to look into 'is eyes,
'E knoo the game clean thro'; 'e seems that wise.
　　Wiv 'er 'an nurse 'e is the leadin' man,
　　An' poor ole dad's amongst the "also ran."

"Goog, goo," 'e sez, and curls 'is cunnin' toes.
Yeh'd be su'prised the 'eaps o' things 'e knows.
　　I'll swear 'e tumbles I'm 'is father, too;
　　The way 'e squints at me, an' sez "Goog, goo."

Why! 'smornin' 'ere 'is lordship gits a grip
Fair on me finger — give it quite a nip!
　　An' when I tugs, 'e won't let go 'is hold!
　　'Angs on like that! An' 'im not three weeks old!

"Goog, goo," 'e sez. I'll swear yeh never did
In all yer natcheril, see sich a kid.
　　The cunnin' ways 'e's got; the knowin' stare —
　　Ther' ain't a youngster like 'im *anywhere!*

An', when 'e gits a little pain inside,
'Is dead straight griffin ain't to be denied.
　　I'm sent to talk sweet nuffin's to the fowls;
　　While nurse turns 'and-springs ev'ry time 'e 'owls.

But say, I tell yeh straight ... I been thro' 'ell!
The things I thort I wouldn't dare to tell
　　Lest, in the tellin' I might feel again
　　One little part of all that fear an' pain.

It come so sudden that I lorst me block.
First, it was, 'Ell-fer-leather to the doc.,
   'Oo took it all so calm 'e made me curse —
   An' then I sprints like mad to get the nurse.

By gum; that woman! But she beat me flat!
A man's jist putty in a game like that.
   She owned me 'appy 'ome almost before
   She fairly got 'er nose inside me door.

Sweatin' I was! but cold wiv fear inside —
An' then, to think a man could be denied
   'Is wife an' 'ome an' told to fade away
   By jist one fat ole nurse 'oo's in 'is pay!

I wus too weak wiv funk to start an' rouse.
'Struth! Ain't a man the boss in 'is own 'ouse?
   "You go an' chase yerself!" she tips me straight.
   There's nothin' now fer you to do but — wait."

Wait? ... Gawd! ... I never knoo wot waitin' meant
In all me life till that day I was sent
   To loaf around, while there inside — Aw, strike!
   I couldn't tell yeh wot that hour was like!

Three times I comes to listen at the door;
Three times I drags meself away once more;
   'Arf dead wiv fear; 'arf dead wiv tremblin' joy ...
   An' then she beckons me, an' sez — "A boy!"

"A boy!" she sez. "An' bofe is doin' well!"
I drops into a chair, an' jist sez — "'Ell!"
    It was a pray'r. I feels bofe crook an' glad....
    An' that's the strength of bein' made a dad.

I thinks of church, when in that room I goes,
'Oldin' me breaf an' walkin' on me toes.
    Fer 'arf a mo' I feared me nerve 'ud fail
    To see 'er lying there so still an' pale.

She looks so frail, at first, I dursn't stir.
An' then, I leans acrost an' kisses 'er;
    An' all the room gits sorter blurred an' dim ...
    She smiles, an' moves 'er 'ead. "Dear lad! Kiss 'im."

Near smothered in a ton of snowy clothes,
First thing, I sees a bunch o' stubby toes,
    Bald 'ead, termater face, an' two big eyes.
    "Look, Kid," she smiles at me. "Ain't 'e a size?"

'E didn't seem no sorter size to me;
But yet, I speak no lie when I agree;
    "'E is," I sez, an' smiles back at Doreen,
    "The biggest nipper fer 'is age I've seen."

She turns away; 'er eyes is brimmin' wet.
"Our little son!" she sez. "Our precious pet!"
    An' then, I seen a great big drop roll down
    An' fall — kersplosh! — fair on 'is nibs's crown.

An' still she smiles. "A lucky sign," she said.
"Somewhere, in some ole book, one time I read,
   The child will sure be blest all thro' the years
   Who's christened wiv 'is mother's 'appy tears.'"

"Kiss 'im," she sez. I was afraid to take
Too big a mouthful of 'im, fear 'e'd break.
   An' when 'e gits a fair look at me phiz
   'E puckers up 'is nose, an' then — Geewhizz!

'Ow did 'e 'owl! In 'arf a second more
Nurse 'ad me 'ustled clean outside the door.
   Scarce knowin' 'ow, I gits out in the yard,
   An' leans agen the fence an' thinks reel 'ard.

A long, long time I looks at my two 'ands.
"They're all I got," I thinks, "they're all that stands
   Twixt this 'ard world an' them I calls me own.
   An' fer their sakes I'll work 'em to the bone."

Them vows an' things sounds like a lot o' guff.
Maybe, it's foolish thinkin' all this stuff —
   Maybe, it's childish-like to scheme an' plan;
   But — I dunno — it's that way wiv a man.

I only know that kid belongs to me!
We ain't decided yet wot 'e's to be.
   Doreen, she sez 'e's got a poit's eyes;
   But I ain't got much use fer them soft guys.

I think we ort to make 'im something great —
A bookie, or a champeen 'eavy-weight:
   Some callin' that'll give 'im room to spread.
   A fool could see 'e's got a clever 'ead.

I know 'e's good an' honest; for 'is eyes
Is jist like 'ers; so big an' .lovin'-wise;
   They carries peace an' trust where e'er they goes
   An', say, the nurse she sez 'e's got my nose!

Dead ring fer me ole conk, she sez it is.
More like a blob of putty on 'is   phiz,
   I think. But 'e's a fair 'ard case, all right.
   I'll swear I thort 'e wunk at me last night!

My wife an' fam'ly! Don't it sound all right!
That's wot I whispers to meself at night.
   Some day, I s'pose, I'll learn to say it loud
   An' careless; kiddin' that I don't feel proud.

My son! ... If there's a Gawd 'Oos leanin' near
To watch our dilly little lives down 'ere,
   'E smiles, I guess, if 'E's a lovin' one —
   Smiles, friendly-like, to 'ear them words — My son.

XIV.   THE MOOCH O' LIFE

HAL GYE

The Mooch o' Life

 HIS ev'nin' I was sittin' wiv Doreen,
    Peaceful an' 'appy wiv the day's work done,
Watchin', be'ind the orchard's bonzer green,
    The flamin' wonder of the settin' sun.

Another day gone by; another night
Creepin' along to douse Day's golden light;
    Another dawnin', when the night is gone,
    To live an' love — an' so life mooches on.

Times I 'ave thought, when things was goin' crook,
When 'Ope turned nark an' Love forgot to   smile,
    Of somethin' I once seen in some old book
Where an ole sore-'ead arsts, "Is life worf w'ile?"

But in that stillness, as the day grows dim,
An' I am sittin' there wiv 'er an"im —
    My wife, my son! an' strength in me to strive,
    I only know — it's good to be alive!

Yeh live, yeh love, yeh learn; an' when yeh corn
To square the ledger in some thortful hour,
    The everlastin' answer to the sum
Must allus be, "Where's sense in gittin' sour?"

Fer when yeh've come to weigh the good an' bad —
The gladness wiv the sadness you 'ave 'ad —
    Then 'im 'oo's faith in 'uman goodness fails
    Fergit to put 'is liver in the scales.

Livin' an' lovin'; learnin' day be day;
    Pausin' a minute in the barmy strife
To find that 'elpin' others on the way
    Is gold coined fer your profit — sich is life.

I've studied books wiv yearnings to improve,
To 'eave meself out of me lowly groove,
    An' 'ere is orl the change I ever got:
    "'Ark at yer 'eart, an' you kin learn the lot."

I gives it in — that wisdom o' the mind —
    I wasn't built to play no lofty part.
Orl such is welkim to the joys they find;
    I only know the wisdom o' the 'eart.

An' ever it 'as taught me, day be day,
The one same lesson in the same ole way:
    "Look fer yer profits in the 'earts o' friends,
    Fer 'atin' never paid no dividends."

Life's wot yeh make it; an' the bloke 'oo tries
To grab the shinin' stars frum out the skies
Goes crook on life, an' calls the world a cheat,
An' tramples on the daisies at 'is feet.

But when the moon comes creepin' o'er the hill,
An' when the mopoke calls along the creek,
I takes me cup o' joy an' drinks me fill,
An' arsts meself wot better could I seek.

An' ev'ry song I 'ear the thrushes sing
That everlastin' message seems to bring;
    An' ev'ry wind that whispers in the trees
    Gives me the tip there ain't no joys like these:

Livin' an' lovin'; wand'rin' on yer way;
    Reapin' the 'arvest of a kind deed done;
An' watchin', in the sundown of yer day,
    Yerself again, grown nobler in yer son.

Knowin' that ev'ry coin o' kindness spent
Bears interest in yer 'eart at cent per cent;
    Measurin' wisdom by the peace it brings
    To simple minds that values simple things.

An' when I take a look along the way
    That I 'ave trod, it seems the man knows best,
Who's met wiv slabs of sorrer in 'is day,
    When 'e is truly rich an' truly blest.

An' I am rich, becos me eyes 'ave seen
The lovelight in the eyes of my Doreen;
    An' I am blest, becos me feet 'ave trod
    A land 'oo's fields reflect the smile o' God.

Livin' an' lovin'; learnin' to fergive
The deeds an' words of some un'appy bloke
Who's missed the bus — so 'ave I come to live,
An' take the 'ole mad world as 'arf a joke.

Sittin' at ev'nin' in this sunset-land,
Wiv 'Er in all the World to 'old me 'and,
    A son, to bear me name when I am gone ...
    Livin' an' lovin' — so life mooches on.

THE GLOSSARY

The Glossary

A.I.F. — Australian Imperial Force.

Alley, to toss in the. — To give up the ghost.

Also ran, the. — On the turf, horses that fail to secure a leading place; hence, obscure persons, nonentities.

'Ammer-lock (Hammer-lock). — A favourite and effective hold in wrestling.

Ar. — An exclamation expressing joy, sorrow, surprise, etc., according to the manner of utterance.

'Ard Case (Hard Case). —A shrewd or humorous person.

'Ayseed (Hayseed). — A rustic.

Back Chat. — Impudent repartee.

Back and Fill. — To vacillate; to shuffle.

Back the Barrer. — To intervene without invitation.

Barmy (Balmy). — Foolish; silly.

Beak. — A magistrate. (Possibly from Anglo-Saxon, Beag)

Beano. — A feast.

Beans. — Coins; money.

Beat. — Puzzled; defeated.

Beat, off the. —Out of the usual routine.

Beef (to beef it out). —To declaim vociferously.

Bellers (Bellows). — The lungs.

Biff. —To smite.

Bird, to give the. —To treat with derision.

Blighter. — A worthless fellow.

Bli'me. — An oath with the fangs drawn.

Blither. — To talk at random, foolishly.

Blob. — A shapeless mass.

Block. — The head. **To lose or do in the block**. — To become flustered; excited; angry; to lose confidence. **To keep the block.** —To remain calm; dispassionate.

Block, the. —A fashionable city walk.

Bloke. — A male adult of the genus homo.

Blubber, blub. — To weep.

Bluff. — Cunning practice; make believe. v. To deceive; to mislead.

Bob. — A shilling.

Bokays. — Compliments, flattery.

Boko. — The nose.

Bong-tong.— Patrician (Fr. Bon ton).

Bonzer, boshter, bosker.—Adjectives expressing the superlative of excellence.

Boodle.— Money; wealth.

Book.— A bookie, q.v.

Bookie.— A book-maker (turf); one who makes a betting book on sporting events.

Boot, to put in the.— To kick a prostrate foe.

Boss.— Master, employer.

Break (to break away, to do a break).— To depart in haste.

Breast up to.— To accost.

Brisket.— The chest.

Brown.— A copper coin.

Brums.— Tawdry finery (From Brummagem—Birmingham).

Buckley's (Chance).— A forlorn hope.

Buck-up.— Cheer up.

Bump.— To meet; to accost aggressively.

Bun, to take the.— To take the prize (used ironically).

Bundle, to drop the.— To surrender; to give up hope.

Bunk.— To sleep in a "bunk" or rough bed. **To do a bunk.**— To depart.

Bunnies, to hawk the.— To peddle rabbits.

Bus, to miss the.— To neglect opportunities.

Caboose.— A small dwelling.

Carlton.— A Melbourne Football Team.

Cat, to whip the.— To cry over spilt milk; i.e. to whip the cat that has spilt the milk.

C.B.— Confined to barracks.

Cert.— A certainty; a foregone conclusion.

Champeen.— Champion.

Chase yourself.— Depart; avaunt; "fade away," q.v.

Chat.— To address tentatively; to "word" q.v.

Cheque, to pass in one's.— To depart this life.

Chest, to get it off one's.— To deliver a speech; express one's feelings.

Chew, to chew it over; to chew the rag.— To sulk; to nurse a grievance.

Chiack.— Vulgar banter; coarse invective.

Chin.— To talk; to wag the chin.

Chip.— To "chat," q.v.

Chip in.— To intervene.

Chiv.— The face.

Chow.— A native of far Cathay.

Chuck up.— To relinquish. **Chuck off.—** To chaff; to employ sarcasm.

Chump.— A foolish fellow.

Chunk.— A lump; a mass.

Clean.— Completely; utterly.

Click.— A clique; a "push," q.v.

Cliner.— A young unmarried female.

Clobber.— Raiment; vesture.

Cobber.— A boon companion.

Collect.— To receive one's deserts.

Colour-line.— In pugilism, the line drawn by white boxers excluding coloured fighters—for divers reasons.

Conk.— The nose.

Coot.— A person of no account (used contemptuously).

Cop.— To seize; to secure; also s. An avocation, a "job."

Cop (or Copper).— A police constable.

Copper-top.— Red head.

Copper show.— A copper mine.

Count, to take the.— In pugilism, to remain prostrate for ten counted seconds, and thus lose the fight.

Cove.— A "chap" or "bloke," q.v. (Gipsy).

Cow.— A thoroughly unworthy, not to say despicable, person, place, thing, or circumstance. **A fair cow.—** An utterly obnoxious and otherwise unexpressible person, place, thing, or circumstance.

Crack.— To smite. s. A blow.

Crack a boo.— To divulge a secret; to betray emotion.

Crack hardy.— To suppress emotion; to endure patiently; to keep a secret.

Cray.— A crayfish.

Crib.— A dwelling.

Croak.— To die.

Crook.— A dishonest or evil person.

Crook.— Unwell; dishonest; spurious; fraudulent. Superlative, **Dead Crook.**

Crool (cruel) the pitch.— To frustrate; to interfere with one's schemes or welfare.

Crust.— Sustenance; a livelihood:

Cut it out.— Omit it; discontinue it.

Dago.— A native of Southern Europe.

Dash, to do one's.— To reach one's Waterloo.

Date.— An appointment.

Dawg (dog).— A contemptible person; ostentation. **To put on dawg.** — To behave in an arrogant manner.

Dead.— In a superlative degree; very.

Deal.— To deal it out; to administer punishment, abuse, etc.

Deener.— A shilling (Fr. Denier.Denarius, a Roman silver coin).

Derry.— An aversion; a feud; a dislike.

Dickin.— A term signifying disgust or disbelief.

Dile (dial).— The face.

Dilly.— Foolish; half-witted.

Ding dong.— Strenuous.

Dinkum.— Honest; true. **"The Dinkum Oil."**— The truth.

Dirt.— Opprobrium, a mean speech or action.

Dirty left.— A formidable left fist.

Divvies.— Dividends; profits.

Dizzy limit.— The utmost; the superlative degree.

Do in.— To defeat; to kill; to spend.

Done me luck.— Lost my good fortune.

Dope.— A drug; adulterated liquor. v. To administer drugs.

Dot in the eye, to.— To strike in the eye.

Douse.— To extinguish (Anglo-Saxon).

Drive a quill.— To write with a pen; to work in an office.

Duck, to do a.— See "break."

Duds.— Personal apparel (Scotch).

Dunno.— Do not know.

Dutch.— German; any native of Central Europe.

'Eads (Heads).— The authorities; inner council.

'Eadin'.— "Heading browns"; tossing pennies.

'Ead over Turkey.— Head over heels.

'Ead Serang.— The chief; the leader.

'Eavyweight.— A boxer of the heaviest class.

'Ell-fer-leather.— In extreme haste.

End up, to get.— To rise to one's feet.

Fade away, to.— To retire; to withdraw.

Fag.— A cigarette.

Fair.— Extreme; positive;

Fair thing.— A wise proceeding; an obvious duty.

Fake.— A swindle; a hoax.

Finger.— An eccentric or amusing person.

Flam.— Nonsense; make-believe.

Flash.— Ostentatious; showy but counterfeit.

Float, to.— To give up the ghost.

Fluff, a bit of.— A young female person.

Foot (me foot).— A term expressing ridicule.

Footer.— Football.

Frame.— The body.

Frill.— Affectation.

Funk, to.— To fear; to lose courage.

Furphy.— An idle rumour; a canard

Galoot.— A simpleton.

Game.— Occupation; scheme; design.

Gawsave.— The National Anthem.

Gazob.— A fool; a blunderer.

Geewhizz.— Exclamation expressing surprise.

Get, to do a.— To retreat hastily.

Gilt.— Money; wealth.

Give, to.—In one sense, to care.

Gizzard.— The heart.

Glarssy.— The glassy eye; a glance of cold disdain. **The Glassey Alley.**— The favourite; the most admired.

Glim.— A light.

Going (while the going is good).— While the path is clear.

Gone (fair gone).— Overcome, as with emotion.

Goo-goo eyes.— Loving glances.

Gorspil-cove.— A minister of the Gospel.

Graft.— Work.

Grafter.— One who toils hard or willingly.

Griffin, the straight— The truth, secret information.

Grip.— Occupation; employment.

Groggy.— Unsteady; dazed.

Grouch.— To mope; to grumble.

Grub.— Food.

Guff.— Nonsense.

Guy.— A foolish fellow.

Guy, to do a.— To retire.

Guyver.— Make-believe.

Handies.— A fondling of hands between lovers.

Hang out.— To reside; to last.

Hang-over.— The aftermath of the night before.

Hankies.— Handkerchiefs.

High-falutin'.— High sounding; boastful.

Hitch, to.— To wed.

Hitched.— Entangled in the bonds of holy matrimony.

Hit things up.— To behave strenuously; riotously.

Hot.— Excessive, extreme.

Hump, the.— A fit of depression.

Hump, to.— To carry as a swag or other burden.

Imshee.— Begone; retreat; to take yourself off.

Intro.— Introduction; "knock—down," q.v.

It (to be It),— To assume a position of supreme importance.

Jab.— To strike smartly.

Jane.— A woman.

Jiff.— A very brief period.

Job, to.— To smite.

Joes.— Melancholy thoughts.

John.— A policeman.

Joint, to jump the.— To assume command; to occupy the "joint," i.e., establishment, situation, place of business.

Jolt, to pass a.— To deliver a short, sharp blow.

Jor.— The jaw.

Jorb (Job).— Avocation; employment.

Josser.— A simple fellow.

Jug.— A prison.

Keekin'.— Peeping.

Keeps, for.— For ever; permanently.

Kersplosh.— Splash.

Kid.— A child.

Kid, to.— To deceive; to persuade by flattery.

Kiddies.— Children.

Kid Stakes.— Pretence.

King Pin.— The leader; the person of chief importance.

Kip.— A small chip used for tossing pennies in the occult game of two-up.

Kipsie.— A house; the home.

Knob.— The head; one in authority.

Knock-down.— A ceremony insisted upon by ladies who decline to be "picked up"; a formal introduction.

Knock-out drops.— Drugged or impure liquor.

Knock-out punch.— A knock-down blow.

Knut.— A fop; a well-dressed idler.

Lark.— A practical joke; a sportive jest.
Lash.— Violence.
Ledding.— Leaden.
Leery.— Vulgar; low.
Leeuwin.— Cape Leeuwin on the south-west coast of Australia.
Lid.— The hat. **To dip the lid.**— To raise the hat.
Limit.—The end; the full length.
Line up.— To approach; to accost.
Lingo.— Language.
Lip.— Impertinence. **To give it lip.**— To talk vociferously.
Little Bourke.— Little Bourke Street, Melbourne, Australia.
Little Lon.— Little Lonsdale Street, Melbourne, Australia.
Lob, to.— To arrive.
'Loo.—Woolloomooloo, a part of Sydney.
Lumme.— Love me.
Lurk.— A plan of action; a regular occupation.

Mafeesh.— Finish; I am finished.
Mag.— To scold or talk noisily.
Mallee.— A species of Eucalypt; the country where the Mallee grows.
Mash.— To woo; to pay court. s. A lover.
Maul.— To lay hands upon, either violently or with affection.
Meet, a.— An assignation.
Mill.— A bout of fisticuffs.
Mix.— To mix it; to fight strenuously.
Mizzle.— To disappear; to depart suddenly.
Mo.— An abbreviation of "moment."
Moll.— A woman of loose character.
Moniker.— A name; a title; a signature.
Mooch.— To saunter about aimlessly.
Moon.— **To loiter.**
Mud, my name is.— i.e., I am utterly discredited.
Mug.— A fool; also the mouth.
Mug, to.— To kiss.
Mullock, to poke.— To deride; to tease.
Mushy.—Sentimental.

Nark.—s. A spoil-sport; a churlish fellow.

Nark, to.— To annoy; to foil.

Narked.— Angered; foiled.

Natchril.— Natural.

Neck, to get it in the.— To receive severe punishment; i.e., "Where the chicken got the axe."

Nerve.— Confidence; impudence.

Nick.— Physical condition; good health.

Nipper.— A small boy.

Nose around, to.— To seek out inquisitively.

Nothing (ironically).— Literally "something considerable."

Odds, above the.— Beyond the average; outside the pale.

Oopizootics.— An undiagnosed complaint.

Orfis (office).— A warning; a word of advice; a hint.

Oricle (oracle), to work the.— To secure desired results.

Orl (all in).— Without limit or restriction.

'Ot socks.— Gaily-coloured hose.

Out, to.— To render unconscious with a blow.

Out, all.— Quite exhausted; fully extended.

Pack, to send to the.— To relegate to obscurity.

Pal.— A friend; a mate (Gipsy).

Pard.— A partner; a mate.

Pass (pass 'im one).— To deliver a blow.

Pat, on one's.— Alone; single-handed.

Peach.— A desirable young woman; "fresh as a peach."

Peb (pebble).— A flash fellow; a "larrikin."

Phiz.—The face.

Pick at.— To chaff; to annoy.

Pick-up, to.— To dispense with the ceremony of a "knock-down" or introduction.

Pilot Cove.— A clergyman.

Pile it on.— To rant; to exaggerate.

Pinch.—To steal; to place under arrest.

Pip.—A fit of depression.

Pitch a tale.— To trump up an excuse; to weave a romance.

Plant.— To bury.

Plug.— To smite with the fist.

Plug along, to.— To proceed doggedly.

Plunk.—An exclamation expressing the impact of a blow.

Podgy.— Fat; plump.

Point.— The region of the jaw; much sought after by pugilists.

Point, to.— To seize unfair advantage; to scheme.

Pole, up the.— Distraught through anger, fear, etc.; also, disappeared, vanished.

Pot, a.— A considerable amount; as a "pot of money."

Pot, the old. — The male parent (from "Rhyming Slang,") the "old pot and pan — the old man.

Prad.— A horse.

Pug.— A pugilist.

Pull, to take a.— To desist; to discontinue.

Punch a cow.— To conduct a team of oxen.

Punter.— The natural prey of a "bookie," q.v.

Push.— A company of rowdy fellows gathered together for ungentle purposes.

Queer the pitch.— To frustrate; to fool.

Quid.— A sovereign, or pound sterling.

Quod.— Prison.

Rabbit, to run the.—To convey liquor from a public house.

Rag, to chew the.— To grieve; to brood.

Rag, to sky the.— To throw a towel into the air in token of surrender (pugilism).

Rain, to keep out of the.— To avoid danger; to act with caution.

Rat.— A street urchin; a wharf loafer.

Rattled.— Excited; confused.

Red 'ot.— Extreme; out-and-out.

Registry.— The office of a Registrar.

Ribuck.— Correct, genuine; an interjection signifying assent.

Rile.—To annoy. **Riled.**— Roused to anger.

Ring, the.— The arena of a prize-fight.

Ring, the dead.— A remarkable likeness.

Rise, a.— An accession of fortune; an improvement.

Rocks.— A locality in Sydney.

Rorty.— Boisterous; rowdy.

Roust, or Rouse.— To upbraid with many words.

'Roy.— Fitzroy, a suburb of Melbourne; its football team.

Run against.— To meet more or less unexpectedly.

Saints.— A football team of St Kilda, Victoria.

Sandy blight.— Ophthalmia.

Savvy.— Commonsense; shrewdness.

School.— A club; a clique of gamblers, or others.

Scran.— Food.

Scrap.— Fight.

Set, to.— To attack; to regard with disfavour.

Set, to have.— To have marked down for punishment or revenge.

Shick, shickered.— Intoxicated.

Shicker.— Intoxicating liquor.

Shinty.— A game resembling hockey.

Shook.— Stolen; disturbed.

Shook on.— Infatuated.

Shyin' or Shine.— Excellent; desirable.

Sight.— To tolerate; to permit; also to see; observe.

Sir Garneo.— In perfect order; satisfactory.

Skirt or bit of skirt.— A female.

Skite.— To boast. **Skiter.**— A boaster.

Sky the wipe.— See "rag."

Slab.— A portion; a tall, awkward fellow.

Slanter.— Spurious; unfair.

Slap-up.— Admirable; excellent.

Slats.— The ribs.

Slaver.— One engaged in the "white slave traffic."

Slick.— Smart; deft; quick.

Slope, to.— To elope; to leave in haste.

Sloppy.— Lachrymose; maudlin.

Slushy.— A toiler in a scullery.

Smooge.— To flatter or fawn; to bill and coo.

Smooger.— A sycophant; a courtier.

Snag.— A hindrance; formidable opponent.

Snake-'eaded.— Annoyed, vindictive.

Snake juice.— Strong drink.

Snare.— To acquire; to seize; to win.

Snide.— Inferior; of no account.

Snob. — A bootmaker.

Snout. — To bear a grudge.

Snouted.— Treated with disfavour.

Snuff or snuff it.— To expire.

Sock it into.— To administer physical punishment.

Solid.— Severe; severely.

So-long.— A form of farewell.

Sool.— To attack; to urge on.

Soot, leadin'.— A chief attribute.

Sore, to get.— To become aggrieved.

Sore-head.— A curmudgeon.

Sour, to turn, or get.—— To become pessimistic or discontented.

Spank.— To chastise maternal-wise.

Spar.— A gentle bout of fisticuffs.

Spare me days.— A pious ejaculation.

Specs.— Spectacles.

Splash.— To expend.

Splice.— To join in holy matrimony.

Spout.— To preach or speak at length.

Sprag.— To accost truculently.

Spruik.— To deliver a speech, as a showman.

Square.— Upright, honest.

Square an' all.— Of a truth; verily.

Squiz.— A brief glance.

Stand-orf.— Retiring; reticent.

Stajum.— Stadium, where prize-fights are conducted.

Stiffened.— Bought over.

Stiff-un.— A corpse.

Stoke.— To nourish; to eat

Stop a pot.— To quaff ale.

Stoush.— To punch with the fist. s. Violence.

Straight, on the.— In fair and honest fashion.

Strangle-hold.— An ungentle embrace in wrestling.

Strength of it.— The truth of it; the value of it.

Stretch, to do a.— To serve a term of imprisonment.

Strike.— The innocuous remnant of a hardy curse.

Strike.— To discover; to meet.

Strong, going.— Proceeding with vigour.

'Struth.— An emaciated oath.

Stuff.— Money.

Stunt.— A performance; a tale.

Swad, Swaddy.— A private soldier.

Swank.— Affectation; ostentation.

Swap.— To exchange.

Swell.— An exalted person.

Swig.— A draught of water or other liquid.

Tabbie.— A female.

Take 'em on.— Engage them in battle.

Take it out.— To undergo imprisonment in lieu of a fine.

Tart.— A young woman (contraction of sweetheart).

Tenner.— A ten-pound note.

Time, to do.— To serve a term in prison.

Time, to have no time for.— To regard with impatient disfavour.

Tip.— To forecast; to give; to warn.

Tip.— A warning; a prognostication; a hint.

Tipple.— Strong drink; to indulge in strong drink.

Toff.— An exalted person.

Togs.— Clothes.

Togged.— Garbed.

Tom.— A girl.

Tony.— Stylish.

Took.— Arrested; apprehended.

Top, off one's.— Out of one's mind.

Top off, to.— To knock down; to assault.

Toss in the towel—See "rag."

Touch.— Manner; mode; fashion.

Tough.— Unfortunate; hardy; also a "tug," q.v.

Tough luck.— Misfortune.

Track with.— To woo; to "go walking with."

Treat, a.— Excessively; abundantly.

Tucked away.— Interred.

Tug.— An uncouth fellow; a hardy rogue.

Tumble to, or to take a tumble.— To comprehend suddenly.

Turkey, head over.— Head over heels.

Turn down.— To reject; dismiss.

Turn, out of one's.— Impertinently; uninvited.

Twig.— To observe; to espy.

Two-up School— A gambling den.

Umpty.— An indefinite numeral.

Upper-cut.— In pugilism, an upward blow.

Uppish.— Proud.

Up to us.— Our turn; our duty.

Vag, on the.— Under the provisions of the Vagrancy Act.

Wallop.— To beat; chastise.

Waster.— A reprobate; an utterly useless and unworthy person.

Waterworks, to turn on the.— To shed tears.

Welt.— A blow.

Wet, to get.—To become incensed; ill-tempered.

Whips.— Abundance.

White (white man).— A true, sterling fellow.

White-headed hoy.— A favourite; a pet.

Willin'.— Strenuous; hearty.

Win, a.— Success.

Wise, to get.— To comprehend; to unmask deceit.

Wolf.— To eat.

Word.— To accost with fair speech.

Wot price.—Behold; how now!

Yakker.— Hard toil.

Yap.— To talk volubly.

Yowling.— Wailing; caterwauling.